Hollis

Für Anette

Danke für Deine Freundschaft.

Lucie

For Valentin and for all children.
May this book encourage you on your food journey.

* YOU SAY: BRACK-ee-oh-SAW-rus

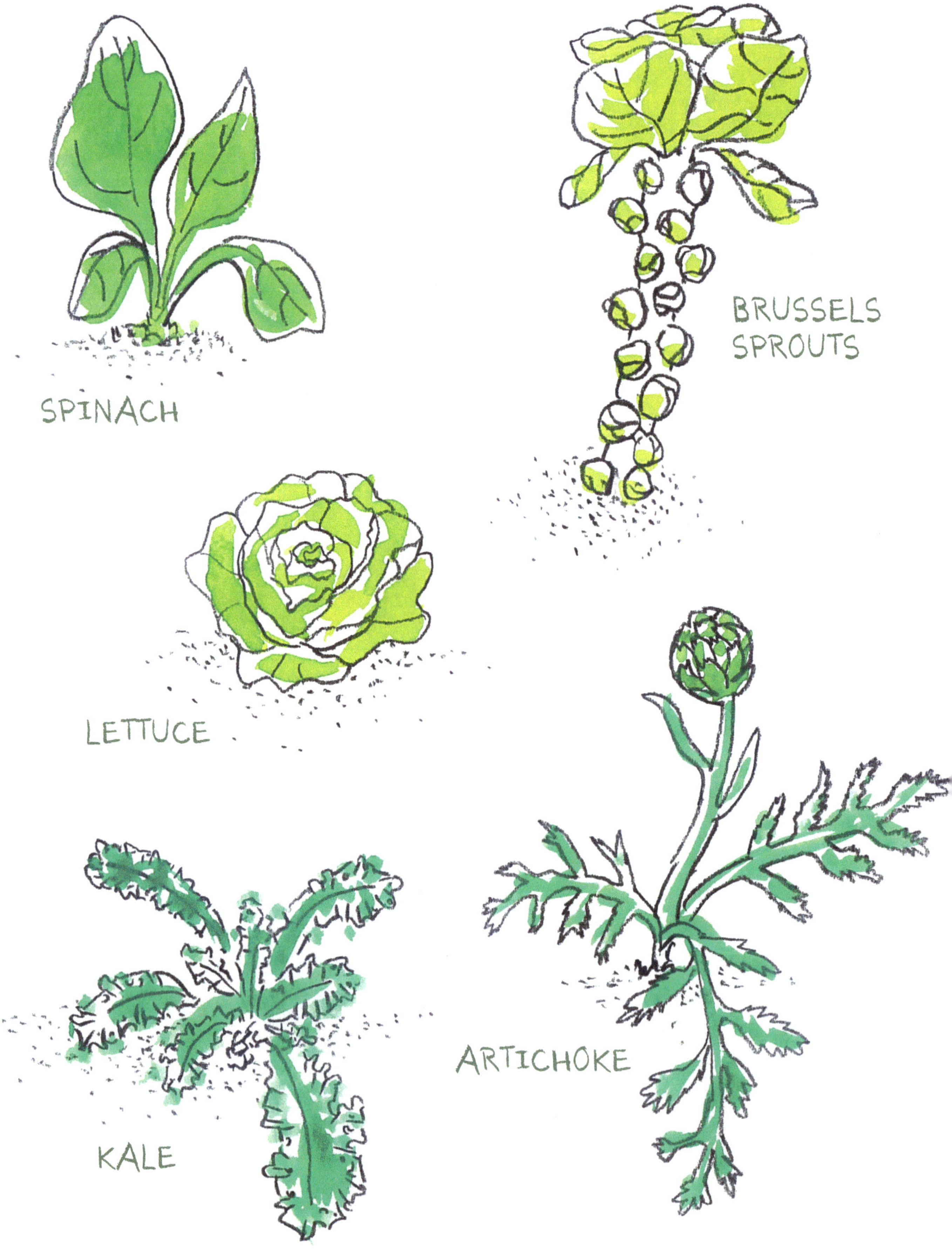
SPINACH
BRUSSELS SPROUTS
LETTUCE
ARTICHOKE
KALE

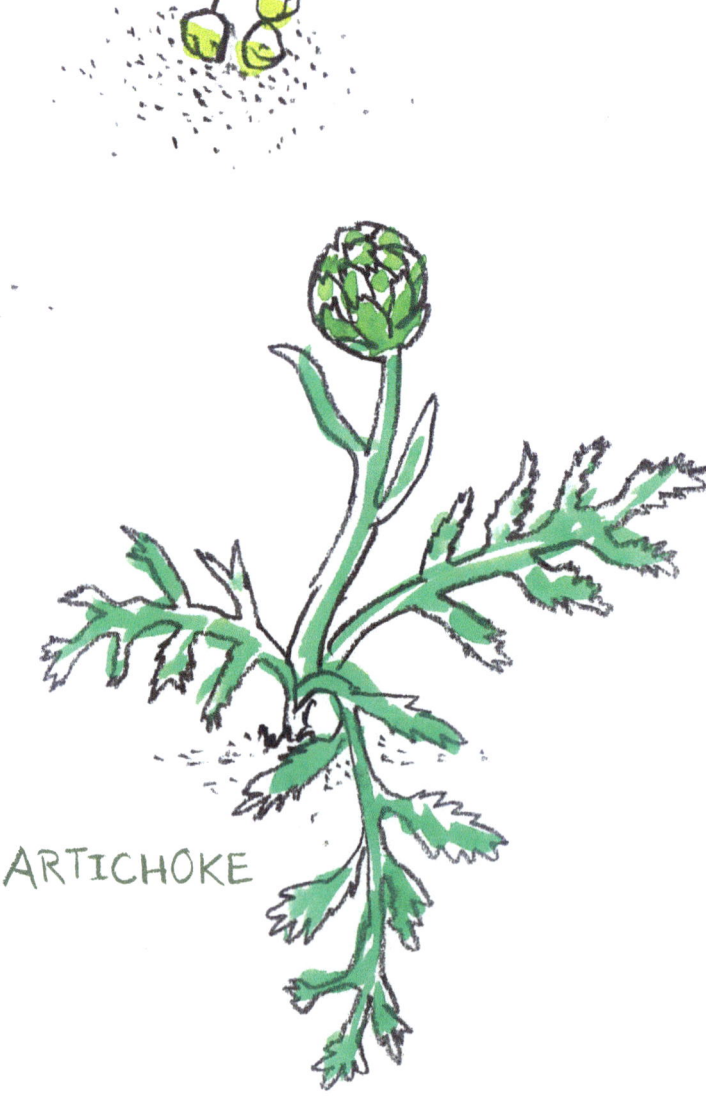

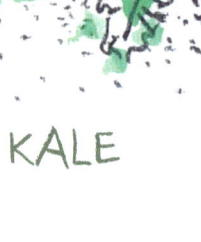

IF BRACHIOSAURUS WERE STILL ALIVE,
THESE ARE THE PLANTS THAT WOULD HELP HIM THRIVE.

*YOU SAY: Nof-ron-e-kus

NOTHRONYCHUS* SAYS:

DO YOU KNOW
MY FAVORITE FOODS?
I LIKE TASTY
VEGGIE ROOTS.

THE ROOTS ARE GROWING
UNDERGROUND,
WAITING LIKE TREASURES
TO BE FOUND.

THESE VEGGIES GIVE ME
THE POWER I NEED,
FROM THE TOP OF MY HEAD,
DOWN TO MY FEET.

ICHTHYOSAURUS* SAYS:

AS A MARINE REPTILE, I LIVE IN THE SEA.
I SWIM ALL DAY, SO WILD AND FREE.

I'M HUNGRY AND HAVE JUST ONE WISH:
TO EAT A LOT OF DELICIOUS FISH!

* YOU SAY: IK-thee-oh-SAW-rus

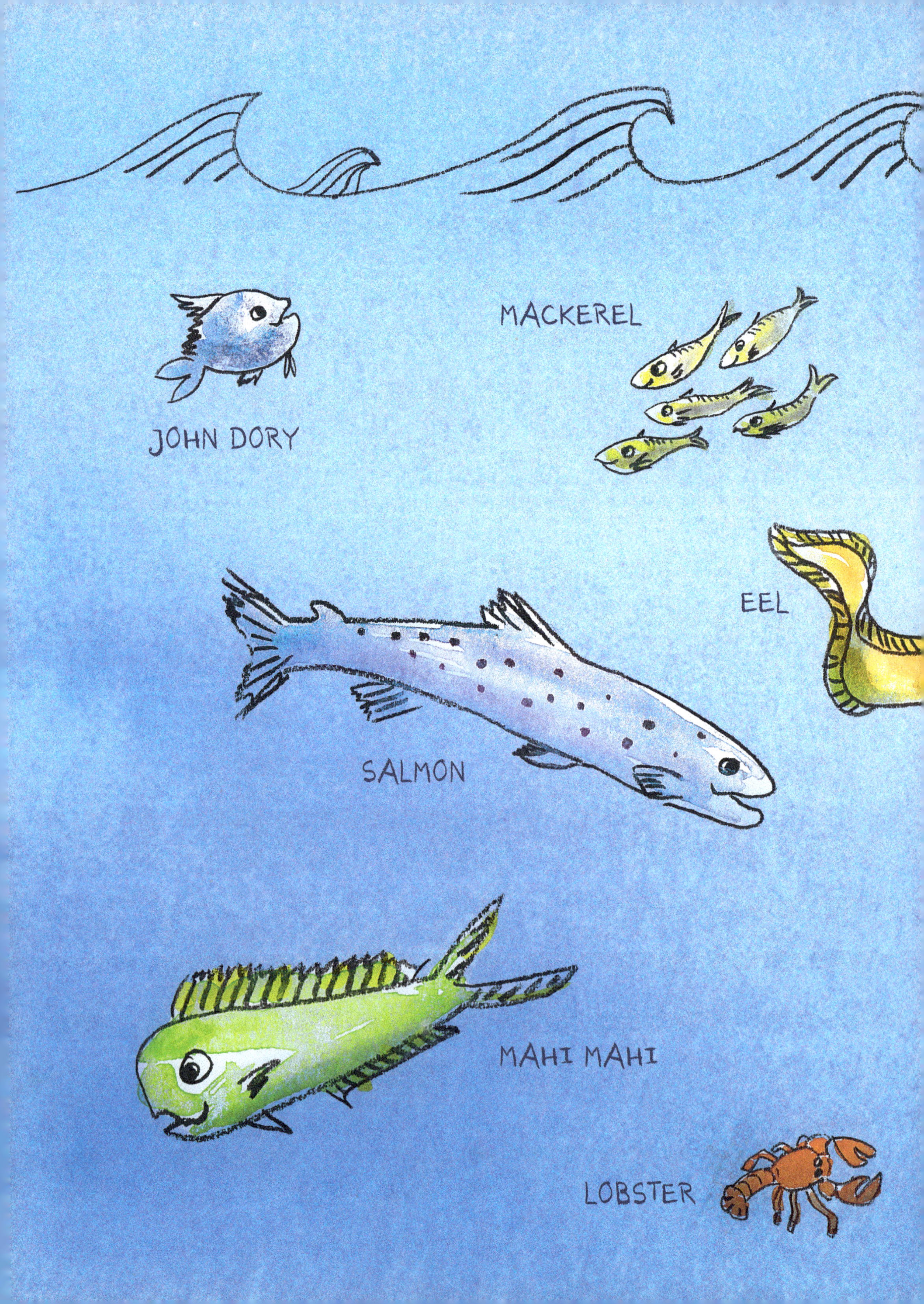
MACKEREL
JOHN DORY
EEL
SALMON
MAHI MAHI
LOBSTER

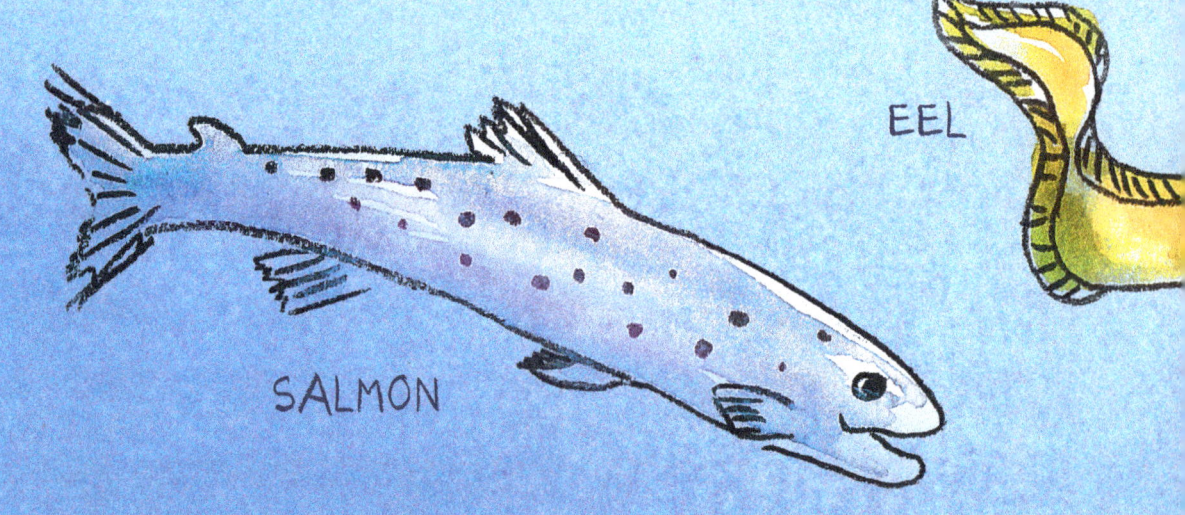

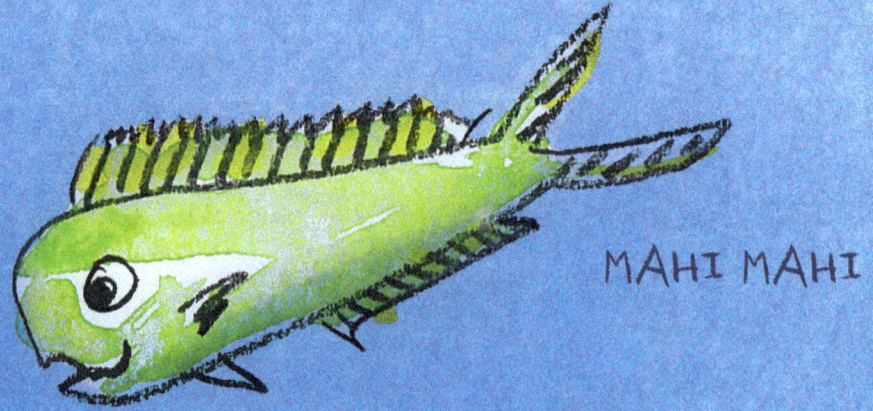

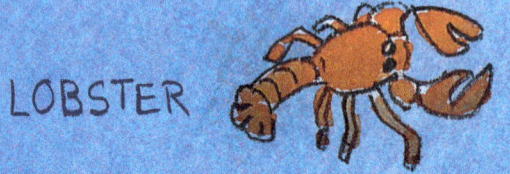

* YOU SAY: SIT-e-ke-SOR-us

PSITTACOSAURUS* SAYS:

EVERY DAY,
NO MATTER MY MOOD,
IT MAKES ME HAPPY
TO TRY NEW FOOD.

MY FAVORITE SNACKS
ARE CRUNCHY SEEDS,
AND ALL KINDS OF PLANTS,
INCLUDING WEEDS.

EVEN THE TINIEST
NUTS I PEEK,
I GRIND THEM WITH
THE BONES OF MY CHEEK.

IF PSITTACOSAURUS WALKED THROUGH THE WOODS TODAY,
HE MIGHT LIKE TO MUNCH THESE ON HIS WAY.

TYRANNOSAURUS* SAYS:

WHETHER AT NIGHT OR IN THE MIDDAY HEAT,
I SNEAK AROUND AND HUNT FOR MEAT.

I HAVE A POWERFUL, DELICATE NOSE,
AND SMELL MY LUNCH FROM FAR AND CLOSE.

ALL CREATURES RUN AWAY AND FLEE,
TRYING TO HIDE IN FRONT OF ME.

* YOU SAY: tie-RAN-oh-SAW-rus

IF TYRANNOSAURUS WERE HUNTING HERE, MAYBE HE'D LOOK FOR A GOOSE OR A DEER.

DUCK

COW

GOOSE

LAMB

THE ORNITHOMIMUS* SAYS:

IN THE BUSHES AND THE SKIES,
I FIND SNACKS WITH MY BIG EYES.

FRUITS AND HERBS, AND EVEN MEAT,
I LIKE ALL FLAVORS; BITTER TO SWEET.

THE RAINBOW COLORS I LOVE TO CHEW
FROM GREEN TO YELLOW, RED AND BLUE.

*You say: or-NITH-oh-MEEM-us

* YOU SAY: STEG-oh-SAW-rus

Stegosaurus (herbivore) had a double row of bony plates on its back, some measuring up to 24 inches (60 cm) high. Its heavy tail was armed with spikes up to 3.25 ft (1 m) long.

Brachiosaurus (herbivore) may have weighed 88 tons (88 tonnes), which is more than 12 African elephants. It probably fed like a giraffe, reaching up to eat leaves on the highest trees.

Ornithomimus (omnivore) is a typical ostrich dinosaur and was 11.5 ft (3.5m) long. It had no teeth but it used its hard beak to chop its food into pieces that it could swallow.

A PLANT EATER LOVES
TO EAT PLANTS
AND NOT MORE.
HIS SCIENTIFIC NAME
IS HERBIVORE.

A MEAT EATER PREFERS
EATING MEAT, FOR SURE.
HE IS CALLED
A CARNIVORE.

AND THERE IS
EVEN A DINOSAUR,
WHO EATS PLANTS
AND MEAT:
THE OMNIVORE.

NOW, IN CASE YOU AND A DINOSAUR MEET, YOU KNOW WHAT EACH CREATURE WOULD EAT.

BUT WHAT ABOUT US?

YOU AND I ARE CALLED HUMAN. WE EAT OUR FOOD WITH SPICES LIKE CUMIN.

WHEN IT COMES TO MEALS WE HAVE A CHOICE. TRY TO DISCOVER YOUR INNER VOICE.

START THE JOURNEY,
TAKE A HIKE IN YOUR BOOTS.
HAVE A CLOSE LOOK
AT VEGGIES AND FRUITS.

WHAT DO YOU SEE?

THEY ARE A BLESSING
FOR YOU AND THE EARTH.
THEY BRING LIFE
IN ABUNDANCE AND WORTH.

GO!
FIND OUT AND LEARN.
A HEALTHY HOME
IS WHAT YOU EARN.

In 2018 Annette and her son started to create this book. It helped them tremendously to adapt to their new diet. They studied *The Dino's Diet* at home, at the playground, at preschool, at the museum and the dinosaur theme park.

More information

You can find further information, activities and more about *The Dino's Diet* at www.annettethurner.com.

Sources

www.dinopedia.fandom.com
www.prehistoric-wildlife.com
www.newdinosaurs.com

The Children's Dinosaur Encyclopedia
Book by New Burlington Books

About Annette Thurner

Born and raised in Germany, Annette is a visual artist, designer and author. Together with her family, she currently resides in California. Annette's art and creative storytelling are inspired by her passion for nature and the healing power of food.

She studied Communication Design at the Munich University of Applied Sciences and has worked as a color- and material designer in the product design and automotive industry in Europe and the United States.

In 2016, Annette started to tell and illustrate stories for her three-year-old son, who was suffering from life-threatening asthma. When conventional medical treatment failed to help, Annette turned to food for healing, inspired by the documentary *Food As Medicine* (by Lenore Eklund). As a result, her son recovered from asthma with great success. He is symptom-free since their diet change in 2018. To educate and encourage her son about the healing power of food and using one's imagination, she began creating children's books about these life-changing topics. Annette hopes that these stories will inspire you, wherever you are on your journey!

Annette's family's life has changed dramatically since food - as a key element for natural health and holistic well-being - became a central focus. Healing foods also help Annette to recover from her post-traumatic stress disorder and autoimmune conditions like Hashimoto's disease. You can find Annette on Instagram @annette.thurner where she is building an uplifting and encouraging community.

Thank you

A special thank you to the filmmaker Lenore Eklund. Your movie *Food As Medicine* has saved the life of my son and my family. Thank you to Andreas. Your love and support made this healing process happen. Thank you to Valentin. Your enthusiasm, love and kindness are wonderful blessings. Thank you, Annette H. You are a true inspiration with your open mind that is constantly looking for the best natural, holistic healthcare available. A tremendous thank you to Cornelia F. Your inspiration and encouragement have moved mountains on this path! Thank you to Gwyneth T. Your invitation to teach children about art gave my life direction. Thank you to my fellow MOPs (mothers of preschoolers). Your friendship and prayers kept me going forward. Thank you to the friends and families who encouraged me and my family on this path! Thank you, dear reader, for purchasing and reading this book! Please leave a review of this book at your online retailer or book community. It is an important contribution, to support independent publishing.
Many thanks!

Copyright © 2020 by Annette Thurner

Author & Illustrator Annette Thurner
Cover and book design by Annette Thurner
Editor Amy Betz

All rights reserved. Thank you for buying an authorized edition of this book and for complying with copyright laws by not reproducing, scanning, or distributing any part of it in any form without prior permission from the publisher.

First published in 2020 by Annette Thurner
www.annettethurner.com

Library of Congress Control Number: 2020921224

ISBN: 978-1-7360255-0-5 (paperback)
ISBN: 978-1-7360255-1-2 (hard cover)
ISBN: 978-1-7360255-2-9 (ebook)

This book is printed with nontoxic soy-based ink. The spine and cover boards used in this book are made from 100% recycled paper. The paper used in this book comes from well-managed forests, from timber that is legally harvested and is not from an endangered species and areas.

This book presents the research and ideas of its author. Neither the publisher nor the author is engaged in rendering professional advice or services to the individual reader. The ideas, procedures, and suggestions contained in this book are not intended as a substitute for consulting with your physician. All matters regarding your health require medical supervision. Neither the author nor the publisher shall be liable or responsible for any loss or damage allegedly arising from information or suggestions in this book. The publisher and the author are not responsible for your specific health or allergy needs that may require supervision. Nor are the publisher and author responsible for any adverse reactions, you may have to the foods contained in the book.

CPSIA information can be obtained
at www.ICGtesting.com
Printed in the USA
BVHW020031040121
596903BV00003B/34